MW01078877

The Princess Doodle Book

Illustrated by the Disney Storybook Artists

A GOLDEN BOOK • NEW YORK

ISBN: 978-0-7364-2695-4
www.randomhouse.com/kids
Printed in the United States of America
10 9 8 7 6 5

Hello, dearie! In this special doodle book, *you* get to be the artist! So pick up your magic wands—I mean your crayons, of course—and get ready to add your own magic to each page.

Cinderella loves her feathered friends.
Can you draw a bird on her finger?

Who is asking Cinderella to dance?
Draw him.

Ariel and Flounder are ready to explore.
Draw a sunken ship.

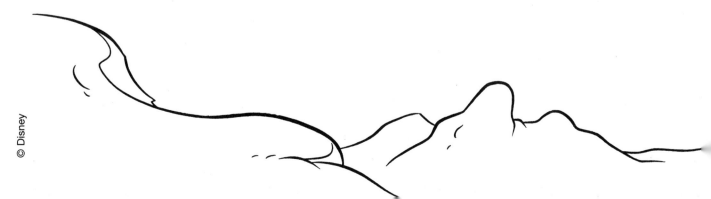

Look at all the treasures Ariel has found!
Can you draw some more?

These birds are placing a crown of flowers on Snow White's head. Can you draw the flowers?

Draw some furry animals to help Snow White clean.

Tiana is a hardworking waitress.
Can you draw some food on her trays?

When Tiana was little, she loved to help her daddy cook.
Draw a stool for little Tiana to stand on.

What a beautiful night!
Can you draw the moon and some stars in the sky?

Chip is excited to eat a yummy dessert.
Draw a sweet treat for him.

Aurora is feeding berries to some birds.
Draw more berries in her basket.

Aurora thinks this dress will be perfect.
Draw a mirror so she can see how it looks.

How does Aladdin reach Jasmine's balcony?
Draw the Magic Carpet for him to ride on.

Rajah's stripes are missing!
Can you draw them?

Who makes Cinderella's dreams come true?
Draw her Fairy Godmother here.

Decorate this invitation.

You Are Invited
to a Royal Ball
at the Castle

Can you draw wheels on Cinderella's carriage?

Sebastian is conducting an underwater orchestra. Draw some singing fish.

Ariel is building a sand castle.
Can you help her?

Draw the rest of Ariel and Prince Eric's wedding cake.

Friendly animals have followed Snow White
to the cottage. Draw some bunnies.

Oh, my!
Draw a poisoned apple in the hand of the wicked Queen.

Tiana wants to wish on the Evening Star.
Can you draw it for her?

Tiana wasn't expecting to meet a frog!
Draw Naveen.

Belle loves to read. Decorate the cover of her book.

Belle is setting Cogsworth to the proper time.
Can you draw his face?

Aurora peeks into a nest.
Fill it with birds and eggs.

The tops of the good fairies' hats are missing.
Can you draw them?

Draw a large jewel at the center of Jasmine's necklace.

Add pretty bows to Cinderella's dress.

Cinderella has lost her glass slipper!
Can you draw it on her foot?

Ariel is in love with Prince Eric.
Draw a heart around him.

Ariel is looking for Prince Eric's ship.
Can you draw it?

Tiana is a frog!
Draw her reflection in the mirror.

The Beast keeps the magic rose safe under this glass.
Can you draw the flower?

Aurora likes to pretend with her friends.
Draw a hat for the squirrel to wear.

Jasmine and Aladdin want to share
a magical moment in the shade.
Draw a tree for them.

Cinderella wants to go to a royal ball.
Draw an invitation for her to hold.

Draw Jaq in Cinderella's hand.

Draw a fork—or a dinglehopper—in Scuttle's wing.

The Little Mermaid lives in Atlantica.
Draw the underwater kingdom.

Snow White loves the smell of flowers.
Add some roses to this bush.

The Seven Dwarfs work hard in the mine.
Draw some diamonds in their sacks.

Tiana and Naveen want to float away.
Draw some balloons.

Draw a shopkeeper waving to Belle from his doorway.

Aurora is making a cake.
Can you help her decorate it?

The Genie can make anything magically appear.
What would you wish for? Draw it here.

Cinderella's stepmother makes her work very hard.
Add a teapot and a cup to each tray.

Ariel wants to wish upon a star.
Draw a big shining star in the sky.

Add balloons to Ariel's and Sebastian's strings.

Two Dwarfs are missing.
Can you draw Sneezy and Bashful?

Snow White has some birdseed in her hands.
Draw birds for her to feed.

Uh-oh! Who is trying to eat the frogs?
Draw another alligator.

Draw Belle's favorite flowers in this bouquet.

Gaston thinks he is very handsome.
Draw his reflection in the mirror.

Add some jewels to Aurora's tiara.

Jasmine loves to fly on the Magic Carpet.
Draw Aladdin sitting next to her.

Draw some ducks for Cinderella to feed.

Who is Ariel kissing?
Draw one of her sea friends.

Ariel has found a pearl!
Draw it inside her shell.

Prince Charming asks Snow White to marry him.
Can you draw Snow White?

Tiana and Naveen meet a nice alligator.
Draw Louis.

Chip likes to sing for his mother.
Draw more musical notes.

Belle and the Beast are having a picnic.
Draw a picnic basket for them.

One of the good fairies is missing.
Can you draw Merryweather?

The Genie always makes Jasmine smile.
Can you draw more balls for the Genie to juggle?

Which vegetables did Cinderella plant?
Draw their pictures on the signs.

Ariel is human!
Draw her feet.

Ariel's family has come to see her get married.
Draw King Triton.

It is dark in the Dwarfs' cottage.
Draw a candle for Snow White to hold.

Watch out for the frog hunters!
Draw their net.

Draw a picture of the Beast in the frame.

Draw some pretty flowers for
Prince Phillip to give to Aurora.

Jasmine flies above the palace.
Can you draw it?

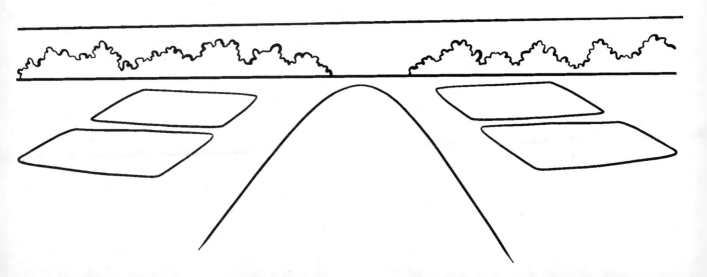

What did Cinderella accidentally
leave behind on the castle steps?
Can you draw it?

Ariel and Flounder are looking for a treasure chest.
Can you draw it?

Snow White likes to cook.
Add some food to the table.

Tiana teaches Naveen how to cook.
Draw a mushroom for him to slice.

Mrs. Potts loves playing with Chip.
Draw a smile on her face.

Aurora is getting married.
Can you draw Prince Phillip?

Jasmine and Aladdin like to monkey around.
Draw Abu.

Cinderella gets ready for her day.
Draw a comb and a mirror on her table.

Ariel and Flounder are following Sebastian.
Draw him.

Draw Flounder swimming through the seaweed ring.

Snow White and her prince are heading home.
Draw their castle.

Who is Snow White so happy to see?

Tiana and Naveen dance.
Draw Ray the firefly overhead.

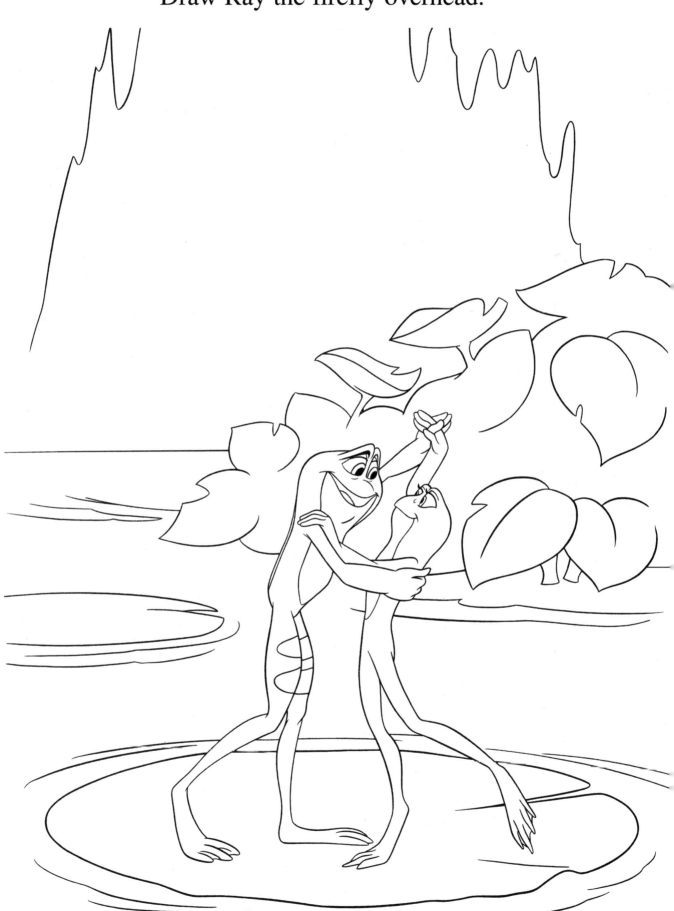

The Beast gets a new look.
Draw some birds fixing his hair.

What does Aurora have in her basket?

Draw flowers in Jasmine's vase.

Draw a basket of apples for Cinderella's horse.

Draw a fancy new hairstyle for Ariel.

Snow White is riding through the forest.
Draw some trees.

Tiana and Naveen enjoy a special dinner.
Draw some food on their table.

Draw dancing forks and spoons.

Draw designs on the royal flags.

Jasmine admires her new headband.
Draw her reflection in the mirror.

Draw a bush for Cinderella's horse to jump over.

Ariel and Flounder have discovered
a room filled with treasure!
Draw more jewels and gold coins.

Ariel is ready to toss her bouquet.
Who is waiting to catch it?

Snow White and the Prince
want to take a walk in the moonlight.
Can you draw the moon?

The Dwarfs are cleaning the house.
Draw something for Dopey to dust.

Tiana and Naveen are getting married!
Can you draw some wedding guests?

Draw Chip sitting in Belle's hands.

Draw more books for Belle to read.

Aurora loves the outdoors.
Draw some trees, flowers, and birds.

Decorate Jasmine's fancy riding outfit.

Jasmine's horse is named Midnight.
Can you decorate Midnight's blanket?

Cinderella is ready for a magical tea party.
Draw a teapot and some snacks.

Who is jumping out of the water to say hi to Ariel?

Draw some undersea friends.

Prince Charming wants to join in the fun.
Can you draw him?

Draw Tiana's wedding veil.

Belle is tossing her bouquet.
Can you draw it?

Aurora is calling to her animal friends.
Can you draw birds and squirrels sitting on the branches?

Can you draw a picture of Rajah hanging on the wall?

What a lovely spring day!
Draw plants and flowers around Cinderella.

Draw a tiara and a necklace for Cinderella.

The Dwarfs are tossing flowers
at the new bride and groom.
Draw the flowers.

Princess Tiana is a beautiful bride!
Decorate her wedding gown.

Can you draw Lumiere's candles?

Scuttle has come to visit Princess Ariel.
Can you draw him?

Who is Ariel singing to?

Jasmine and Aladdin are married!
Draw the happy couple.

Draw more musical animals to serenade Ariel and Eric.

Ariel loves being a princess.
Draw her castle in the background.